Faithful Friends

Columbus, OH • Chicago, IL • Redmond, WA

The McGraw·Hill Companies

The Independent Reading Books

The ***Independent Reading Books*** are reading books that fill the need for easy-to-read stories for the primary grades. The appeal of these stories will encourage independent reading at the early grade levels.

The stories focus on the Dolch 220 Basic Sight Vocabulary and the 95 Common Nouns. Beyond these lists, the books use about three new words per page.

This series was prepared under the direction and supervision of Edward W. Dolch, Ph.D.

This revision was prepared under the direction and supervision of Eleanor Dolch LaRoy and the Dolch Family Trust.

SRAonline.com

 SRA

Send all inquiries to:
SRA/McGraw-Hill
8787 Orion Place
Columbus, OH 43240-4027

Printed in the United States of America.

ISBN 0-07-602527-6

3 4 5 6 7 8 9 BSF 12 11 10 09 08 07 06 05

The **McGraw·Hill** Companies

Table of Contents

Shep and Skyler

Dogs that look after sheep are very smart dogs. This is the story of two sheepdogs.

One of these sheepdogs, Shep, was very old. His owner bought a younger dog called Skyler to help look after the sheep.

The owner told Shep that he was to show Skyler what he had to do. And the old dog seemed to know this.

Shep showed the young dog how to look after the sheep. Every day the sheep had to be taken to where the grass was green.

When the sun was going down, the sheep had to be brought back to the barn again. When the sheep came back to the barn, Shep seemed to know if one was gone and would go after it.

Sometimes Shep and Skyler took the sheep down the road where the cars were going. But the dogs always kept the sheep on the side of the road. No sheep got hurt or ran away when the dogs were looking after them.

Skyler was a smart dog, and he saw what he must do. Soon Shep began to let the young dog do much of the work.

The dogs were fed every day, but now and then the owner gave each dog a big bone with meat on it. When Skyler had eaten as much meat off his bone as he wanted, he would bury his bone in the ground.

It is hard work to bury a big bone in the ground, so Shep did not bury his bones. But when Shep wanted a bone, he would start digging up Skyler's bone.

What was Skyler to do?

One day the owner saw Skyler burying a bone. He was digging a big, big hole. He put his bone into the hole and put a little dirt over the bone.

Then Skyler went away. The owner did not know why Skyler did this.

Soon Skyler came back. In his teeth he had an old bone with no meat on it. The dog put the old bone into the hole and covered it with dirt.

Soon the owner saw Shep digging in the hole that Skyler had made. Shep came to the old bone, picked it up, and carried it away. He did not know that another bone was still down in the hole covered with the dirt.

In this way, Skyler saved his good bone with the meat on it for himself.

Skyler was a very smart dog.

Achilles

Achilles was a big, strong dog. He was not afraid to fight any dog. But Achilles liked to be talked to only in a kind voice.

You had to call Achilles in a kind voice. If you called the big dog in an angry voice, he would not come to you. He would run the other way.

Achilles did not know how strong he was. It was very hard to take a walk with Achilles. His owner always said, "I put a leash on Achilles's collar, and we go for a walk. But Achilles does not walk with me. He pulls the leash, and I go where Achilles wants to go."

If Achilles wanted to go across the street, he just went across the street. He was so strong that his owner could not hold him back. And you could never tell Achilles he was not a good dog, or he would just run away from you.

One day Achilles and his owner were going for a walk. Achilles was being a good dog as they walked along the street.

Suddenly, Achilles saw across the street a little dog barking at a young man. Away went Achilles. He wanted to see this very little dog who was barking so much.

Achilles pulled his owner across the street so fast that she started to fall. She let go of the leash. And she was very angry.

8

"Achilles! Come here!" said the owner.

Away went Achilles down the street. He was running as fast as he could go.

The young man said, "I will get your dog for you." And he ran down the street as fast as he could go.

The owner ran down the street as fast as she could go, calling, "Achilles, Achilles!"

Some little boys who were playing in the street saw the owner. They ran down the street after her as fast as they could go to see what was going on.

A police officer in the street saw the young man running fast, with the owner following after him. The police officer stopped the young man and wanted to know what was the matter.

The owner came up just then and told the police officer that they were all trying to get Achilles, the big dog. So the police officer went with them.

Away went the young man and the police officer and the owner and the little boys down the street calling, "Achilles, Achilles!"

Achilles had been running away, but he saw another dog. He did not like this dog, and Achilles stopped and barked. The other dog barked too. And all at once there was a dogfight.

Just then, the young man and the police officer and the owner and the little boys came up.

The owner knew that Achilles did not know how strong he was. He could hurt the other dog.

The young man and the police officer were trying to get Achilles away from the dog. But Achilles would not stop fighting.

Then the owner went up to the two fighting dogs. Her voice was very kind.

"Achilles, my good Achilles," she said. "Come, my little friend. Good Achilles. Please come to me."

Everyone stopped. Everyone looked. They all started to laugh. They had never seen anyone try to stop a dogfight like that.

But Achilles heard his owner. She was calling him "good dog." Her voice was very kind.

Achilles always thought of himself as a very "good dog." He let go of the other dog and went to his owner right away.

Alma

Alma was a Seeing Eye dog. She had been trained to look after her owner, Mr. Suarez, who could not see. When Mr. Suarez left the house, Alma went with him. She kept Mr. Suarez on the sidewalk. She took Mr. Suarez across streets. She took care of Mr. Suarez at all times.

Alma and Mr. and Mrs. Suarez were in a room on the top floor of a small hotel. They were resting in the afternoon because that night, Mr. Suarez was to give a talk about the work of Seeing Eye dogs.

Alma could not keep still. The dog walked up and down the hotel room. Then she came to the side of Mr. Suarez's bed and put her cold nose on Mr. Suarez's hand.

Mr. Suarez knew something was the matter. He put the harness on Alma and took her into the hall. Everything seemed to be all right.

Mr. Suarez told Alma to go back to the hotel room. Alma did not want to go back. But she obeyed.

Mr. Suarez started to take the harness off Alma, but Alma barked and barked and pushed Mr. Suarez toward the door. Mr. Suarez did not know what to do.

At last Mr. Suarez called his wife, who had been sleeping. Mrs. Suarez could see and could find out what was the matter.

Now all three went out into the hall. Mr. Suarez smelled smoke at once.

Mrs. Suarez said, "The hall is full of smoke. I cannot see anything."

Mr. Suarez could hardly breathe because of the smoke. And Mrs. Suarez could hardly breathe. They heard people calling, "Fire! Fire!" Mr. Suarez knew his wife's eyes could not help. So he called to Alma and said, "To the door outside."

The dog went down the hall through the smoke. The owner had hold of Alma's harness, and Mrs. Suarez had hold of Mr. Suarez's arm.

Suddenly Alma stopped and barked. Mr. Suarez put out his hand in front of him. They had come to a window.

"Alma has brought us to the fire escape," Mr. Suarez said to his wife. He opened the window.

Mr. Suarez wanted Alma to go out first. "Outside," he said. But Alma would not go. Then Mr. Suarez knew that Alma would not think of going away from him. So Mr. Suarez climbed through the window and out on the fire escape in front of the window. Alma went with him. Then Mrs. Suarez climbed out.

Then they could breathe.

The fire escape went down to a roof. Firefighters were on the roof. They were calling to the people on the fire escape.

Mr. Suarez climbed down the fire escape. It did not go all the way to the roof. So when Mr. Suarez came to the end of it, he had to jump the rest of the way. But he was not hurt.

Firefighters went up the fire escape and got Mrs. Suarez. Alma was left on the fire escape all by herself.

Mrs. Suarez knew that Alma could not come down the fire escape. So she told two firefighters how to pick up the big dog.

"Put one arm under her in back of her front legs. Put another arm under her at her back legs. Then you can carry her without hurting her."

A firefighter went up the fire escape. She picked up Alma and carried her down to the roof.

The firefighters were calling from the ground for the people to get off the roof near the fire. So the firefighters took Mr. and Mrs. Suarez and Alma across the roof to where they would be away from the fire.

Mr. and Mrs. Suarez were saved because Alma found her way through the smoke to the fire escape.

The Captain's Dog

A big ship was carrying many men, women, and children. A storm was blowing on the water. Then something would not work in the ship. The captain could not make the ship go where he wanted it to go.

The high winds of the storm blew the ship toward the shore. Near the shore were great rocks that would break up the ship. The men, women, and children on the ship would be hurt.

On the shore, people stood in the wind and rain of the storm. The ship was not far from the shore. But no one could get out to the ship because the waves were too high.

The people on the shore could shoot a big ball with a rope on it. If they could shoot the ball over the ship, the people on the ship could get the rope. Then the people on the ship could pull the rope and get hold of a very big rope that was tied to it.

The big rope could be tied to the ship. Then a basket could be pulled out to the ship to put the people in. It was the only way the people could get off the ship.

The people on the shore would try to shoot the big ball. But the wind was blowing so hard that they could not get the big ball to go over the ship. The rocks and the high waves were starting to break up the ship.

The captain of the ship had a big black dog that was always with him. The dog seemed to know that something was not right on the ship. She ran up and down and barked and barked. The captain had a thought.

"Come here," said the captain to the big dog. "Maybe you can save us. The men and women cannot get through those waves. Maybe a dog can."

The captain tied a rope to the dog's collar. Then he said, "Swim to the shore. Swim to the shore."

The big dog jumped into the water. The big waves pushed her this way and that. But she kept on swimming.

The people on the ship stood and watched the dog. The people on the shore saw the dog too. They stood and watched.

Sometimes the people could see the big black head of the dog as she was swimming in the water. Sometimes the waves would break over the head of the dog, and she would be gone. But then she would come up again, still swimming.

As the big dog got near the shore, the people were afraid the waves would wash her upon the rocks and she would be hurt.

Some people on the shore wanted to get out into the water to help the dog. But the waves drove them back. As the dog got nearer to the shore, the people saw that she was so tired she could hardly swim. Then a big wave went over her head, and she went down.

The people on the shore went again into the water to save the dog. They got to her. They pulled her to the shore. The big dog was happy to be on the shore. She rested from her swim.

The people on the shore took the rope from the dog's collar. They tied a big rope onto the end of it. And the captain pulled and pulled and got the big rope to the ship.

It did not take long to get the big basket going from the ship to the shore. It was blown by the winds, but it went right over the great high waves. The basket got all the men, women, and children to the shore.

The big black dog had saved them.

Nick, the Sheepdog

Nick was a black sheepdog. He was little for a dog that drives sheep, but he would be called a big dog if he lived in town.

Nick helped his owner and the other sheepdog, Rose, herd sheep out in the mountains of Arizona.

One day, the owner bought a big herd of sheep. She wanted to take the sheep into the hills where there was good grass. The sheep would grow and grow. Then the owner could sell the sheep for more money.

After the owner bought the sheep, she found that there were goats in with the sheep.

The owner had not bought the goats. So the goats had to be taken out of the herd of sheep.

This work was done by Nick and Rose. They picked out the goats one at a time. They ran the goats through a gate into another place.

Soon the goats were all out of the herd of sheep.

Then the dogs began to drive the herd of sheep. For one long day, the herd was driven up into the hills of Arizona.

The owner was heading for a water hole because sheep cannot go too long without water to drink. When they got to the water hole, there was no water in it.

While the herd was resting, some of the sheep smelled water. Five of them started off toward the smell of water. They left the rest of the herd and headed right for a river.

Nick started out after the five sheep, but the sheep got to the river before Nick could get to them.

The river was full of water and was going fast. The fast water was carrying the sheep down the river. One sheep got out on a rock that was in the river. Nick knew the sheep could not get off the rock. So Nick knew he must swim out to the rock. He climbed the rock and pushed the sheep off it.

Then Nick jumped into the river again after that sheep. He got it out of the water. He drove all five sheep away from the river.

This time, the five sheep went up a canyon with steep sides. They could not climb the sides. They got up on some rocks and could not turn around. They did not know how to go on, and they did not know to go back.

Nick had to climb the rocks. He got through the sheep and got ahead of them. Then he made them turn around. Nick got the sheep to go down from the rocks.

At last Nick saw a place where they could get out of the canyon. He drove the five sheep up into this place. Now they were out of the canyon. Nick drove them toward the grass higher up.

The sheep came to another canyon that had a bridge across it. But there was a gate. Nick knew this bridge. He had brought sheep over it before. But the owner was not there to open the gate.

So Nick opened the gate himself. He took the end of the gate with his teeth. Then he pulled it back. The sheep went across the bridge.

As Nick drove the sheep along, they came to some high rocks. From the top of the rocks, a mountain lion jumped down on one of the sheep. The others ran away. But Nick ran up and barked and barked.

The mountain lion knew that when there was a barking dog, more dogs and people were near. The mountain lion did not want to be near people. It turned and ran. The sheep that the lion had jumped on was hurt and could not keep up with the other sheep.

Nick got four of the sheep back to the owner and the herd. But he knew one was left behind. So he went back to get it. It was the sheep that had been hurt by the lion.

Nick had to bark at the sheep again and again to keep it going. At last he got that sheep back to the herd.

The owner gave Nick some food. She told Nick he was a good dog. But Nick just did what any good sheepdog knew had to be done. Nick knew his owner's sheep must be kept together.

Snowbird

Two men, Luke and Beaver, lived in Alaska. They worked in the cold bringing supplies from stores to houses far away.

Luke and Beaver used snowshoes to walk in the snow. As they walked, they had to carry the supplies on their backs.

Once they were walking back after carrying supplies to a house far off in the hills. Their snowshoes helped them walk, but it was snowing, and they could not see well.

As they walked, the men heard a dog barking. They knew that something was not right. They ran to where the barking came from and found that a big wolf was fighting a black dog.

Luke got the wolf to go away, but the wolf had hurt the dog.

When the men got to the dog, they found that it was a mother dog. She was hurt, but she knew the men were friends. She took them to where there were two puppies. One puppy was white and one puppy was black.

The mother had been trying to keep the wolf away from her puppies. But she knew that the men were friends, and that they would not hurt her puppies. She got down on the snow and cried. She was trying to tell the men that she was too hurt to care for her puppies.

Luke and Beaver took the mother dog and her puppies back to the small town where they lived. The puppies were so small that their eyes were not open.

The men had some milk, and they fed the puppies. They took care of the mother dog too. They kept her and her puppies very warm.

Day by day, the mother dog got a little better. And her puppies grew and grew! The white puppy was called Snowbird. The black puppy was called Lucky.

Luke and Beaver liked the dogs very much. They liked to play with Snowbird and Lucky. They were very happy to have the puppies.

The two men had to do their work every day. They had to carry many supplies. They had to go from the store to many houses far, far away. It was hard to take good care of the puppies and to keep them warm.

Luke and Beaver had a small sled that they pulled. But they could not put the puppies on the sled. The puppies would be too cold. So the men made little pouches for the puppies. They put these pouches under their coats.

Luke carried Snowbird and Beaver carried Lucky. Each man had a puppy in a pouch under his coat. In the coats the puppies could not put their heads out and get them cold.

Once the men went to an Inuit village with their supplies. The Inuits came out to see the puppies. Snowbird was all white, with blue eyes. Lucky was all black, with brown eyes. The Inuits looked and looked at them.

Snowbird and Lucky grew to be big, strong dogs.

When their mother was well again, Luke and Beaver gave her to a friend. But they wanted to keep Snowbird and Lucky and show them how to pull a sled.

In Alaska at that time, the best way to get from place to place was by sled. A sled pulled by dogs could go over snow, through woods, and along rivers.

The sled Snowbird and Lucky pulled was small. A lot of men used a big sled. It had to have many dogs to pull it. Men with this kind of sled would give a lot of money for big dogs like Snowbird and Lucky.

Luke and Beaver would not take a lot of money. They would always keep their dogs.

One day Luke and Beaver thought they would go over the mountains to find a river in Alaska that was very far away. They were told they could not do it, but they wanted to try. So they started.

For many days the two men, their two dogs, and the sled went higher and higher into the mountains. The wind blew and blew. They got very tired. Their food was all gone. The way was much longer than the men had thought.

Snowbird went on and on, but Lucky was not as strong. He could not go on pulling the sled. He could not go on without food. And so he had to be pulled in the sled by Snowbird.

The sled, pulled only by Snowbird, went on and on. The men ran with the sled. At last they began to go back down the mountain. The men found some food and gave some to Lucky and Snowbird. At last they could get out of the wind and rest.

After a long time the men and the dogs got to the river they had wanted to find. There were towns there and people who could give them food.

Lucky was better after he got some warm food and rest. But Luke and Beaver could see that Lucky did not want to pull a sled through the cold snow any longer. They made him their watchdog and let him live always at their house.

But Snowbird was now a great sled dog. And soon people all over Alaska had heard the story of this big, strong dog.

Sandy

Big Mike was a man who took the letters from one village in Alaska to another. He had many good sled dogs. A sled pulled by dogs was the best way to go from place to place over the snow.

As soon as Big Mike saw Snowbird he wanted to buy him. Big Mike said he would give Luke a lot of money for his big dog with blue eyes. But Luke would not sell Snowbird.

Then Luke found he had to go away from Alaska for a time. So he said he would not sell Snowbird to Big Mike, but he would let Big Mike keep Snowbird for him while he was gone.

Big Mike had to say he would be very good to Snowbird.

Big Mike gave Snowbird the name "Sandy" because the big dog's coat was turning a light yellow.

And "Sandy" was a much better name to call out when Big Mike called to his dogs as they pulled the sled.

Sandy was so big and strong that he was made the lead dog of Big Mike's team of sled dogs. The lead dog has to be very smart. It has to pick the way to go because there are no roads over the snow. The lead dog has to keep all the other dogs pulling as they go after it.

Then, too, the lead dog has to keep the other dogs from fighting.

Sandy was very big and strong, but he did not like to fight. When two of the sled dogs would start to fight, Sandy would watch them. Then, just at the right time, he would run and jump at them. They would be so afraid that they would stop fighting.

There was one time when Sandy would not obey Big Mike.

It was almost the time of the "long night" when the sun hardly comes up at all. Big Mike was going across the hills to a village. It was a new trail for the man and his team of sled dogs.

It was almost dark when Sandy suddenly stopped. The dogs and sled stopped behind him.

"Mush!" cried Big Mike. Big Mike said "Mush" when he wanted Sandy to go ahead. But Sandy would not move.

The dogs had been going all day, and Big Mike thought that maybe the dogs were too tired. So Big Mike stopped for the night. He fed the dogs right there.

In the morning it was time to start, but it was still very dark. Big Mike wanted to get going. He harnessed the dogs.

"Mush!" cried Big Mike.

But Sandy would not move. He stood still. He would not go on.

Big Mike was very angry. Again, Sandy had not obeyed him.

"Mush!" cried Big Mike again. But Sandy did not move.

Then Big Mike got out of the sled. It was so dark that he could hardly see Sandy at the head of the team of dogs. But Big Mike went up to where Sandy stood in the snow.

Just as Big Mike got to Sandy, his feet went out from under him. He started to go down a steep hill that he had not seen.

Sandy jumped and got hold of Big Mike's coat with his teeth. He pulled back, and all the other dogs pulled back. They seemed to know they could all be pulled over the hill.

The dogs pulled and pulled. Big Mike got back up the steep hill. He got to his feet.

After that, Big Mike always knew that Sandy would be right. Sandy was a good lead sled dog.

The Race

Big Mike and his dog team had to go to Nome. In Nome Big Mike found that there was going to be a big race. The best dogs from all over Alaska had been brought to Nome for the race.

One of the people who was to have a team in the race was Amy Green. As soon as Amy saw Sandy in Big Mike's team, she wanted to buy Sandy to be her lead dog in the race.

"Sandy is not my dog," said Big Mike. "He is Luke's dog. I cannot sell him."

"I must have Sandy as my lead dog in the big race," said Amy. "I will take good care of him. If you let me have him just for the race, I will take care of all your dogs while you are in Nome."

At last, Big Mike let Amy have Sandy to be her lead dog in the race.

The race was to be from Nome to a town called Candle and then back to Nome. It was a little more than 400 miles in all. And there were to be eight teams in the race.

The day of the race, a blizzard began. But Sandy had gone many miles through many blizzards.

Amy's team was to go first. This was not good, because the first team had to make the trail the others would follow. But Amy was not afraid. She was sure she could keep ahead of the others.

"Mush!" called Amy, and away the dogs went. On and on through the blizzard they went. On and on they went.

The race began at ten in the morning, and the dogs ran all that day. In the afternoon, they had gone more than 70 miles. Amy let the dogs rest, and she fed them. Then they went on again through the snow. No one had run as fast as them.

All night long the dogs kept going. Every few hours they would rest a little while. Amy would go along the team and talk to each dog, calling it by name. She would look at their feet to be sure they were not hurt.

Sandy seemed to know that every dog must run as fast as he could and keep on going. When the day came the dogs ran all morning. They rested now and then and were given something to eat.

In the afternoon they got to Candle ahead of all the other teams. But they had to have some rest.

Amy went to sleep for four hours. When she got up, she found that another team had come to Candle and had started back.

Amy took time to take good care of her dogs and talk to them. She fed them and then harnessed them to the sled. But while Amy did this, three more dog teams had made it to Candle and had started back ahead of them.

"Mush!" called Amy, and she and her dogs started off on the trail to Nome. This time they could follow where the other teams had run in the snow. But Amy's team could not come up behind another team and go by them. If they did this, the dogs would be sure to have a great fight. So when Amy knew that a team was ahead of hers, she told Sandy to make a new trail so they could get around the other team and get ahead of them. This made the trail longer.

At last Amy knew she was ahead of all the other teams. Now they must keep ahead of them. All day and all night the dogs had run for many hours with just a few stops to rest and eat. The dogs were very tired. Amy was very tired too.

The blizzard was blowing harder and harder. Amy knew that if she stopped again, the dogs were so tired that they would all go to sleep and not want to go on.

Sandy seemed to know this. He kept going. Amy talked to her dogs. She could hardly see them because her eyes were almost covered with snow.

Sandy ran on and on. He had cut his feet on the trail. He left red places on the snow as he ran on and on.

Three days after they had started, Amy and her team of dogs got back to Nome ahead of all the others. They had come in first in the race. Amy and the dogs were so happy.

Everyone in Alaska knew about Sandy, the lead dog. The papers told the story of the race. Luke, who had just come back, was very happy. His dog came back to him, and they were together again.

Leslie and Whiskers

Ling stood on his red snowboard on top of the mountain. From there the houses of Winter City looked like little toys. This was great! Ling liked being up on the mountain. And he liked to use his snowboard to race down the mountain.

But something was not right. There were no other people on the mountain. And when he looked down at Winter City Ski Lodge, he could not see people around.

"Maybe a storm is near," Ling thought. "I had better go down fast."

Soon Ling was going as fast as he could down the mountain on his snowboard. He turned and jumped, left and right. Suddenly, Ling heard a rumble behind him. The people in Winter City heard it too. The rumble came from a wave of snow and rocks that was falling down the mountain. It was an avalanche! Ling did not know if he could get down the mountain in time to get away!

In a small house by Winter City Ski Lodge, Leslie Briggs and her dog Whiskers heard the rumble. Leslie opened the door to look up the mountain. She saw the wave of rocks and snow as it came down the side.

The avalanche took big and small trees with it. It came down very fast but stopped suddenly on a place on the mountain that stuck out a little.

"Whiskers," she said, "the avalanche is over. It is time to go to work."

Whiskers was trained to find people stuck under the snow after an avalanche. He could find people very fast.

Leslie and Whiskers ran out. Other people were out now too. They were looking at something red stuck in the snow on the mountain.

"Leslie, there is a red snowboard stuck in the snow on the mountain," called a man.

Leslie and Whiskers jumped on a snow tractor. Leslie drove the tractor up the mountain. She stopped a few feet from the red snowboard. Leslie turned the tractor off and put her hand up to see which way the wind was blowing. She then walked Whiskers to one side of the snowboard and put her hand on his back. "Whiskers!" she said. "Go! Find!"

Leslie and Whiskers had trained together for a long time. When Whiskers heard "Go! Find!" he put his nose to the snow and started to sniff. Whiskers was trained to find people by their smell. He could sniff to find the smells under the snow. Soon Whiskers started to sniff one place hard. He barked and started digging in the snow.

Leslie ran to Whiskers and called, "Good dog!" Whiskers barked and kept digging. Leslie was digging too. She and Whiskers made a very big hole.

Then Leslie saw something blue in the hole. It was a coat. Leslie put her hand on the coat. There was an arm in the coat. It was warm! Leslie called, "Good dog, Whiskers. Stop!" Whiskers stopped digging and started barking.

Leslie kept digging. With her hand, she started to clean snow from a young boy's head. The boy was Ling!

Another snow tractor had been coming fast up the mountain. It stopped where Whiskers was barking. Two people jumped out and helped dig. Soon Ling was in the back of the tractor and on the way down to Winter City.

Ling was hurt, but he would soon get better. And thanks to Leslie and Whiskers, he would soon be back on his snowboard again.

Jonathan's Best Friends

Jonathan wanted a dog. It did not have to be a big dog or a little dog—any dog would do. But the apartment that Jonathan, Mama, and his two big sisters lived in was small.

"Jonathan," Mama would say, "I know you would like a dog. But I just don't see how we can get one more thing into this apartment."

"I know, Mama," said Jonathan. And he did know. The apartment was small. But Jonathan still wished he had a dog.

Sometimes his big sisters, Toni and Valerie, thought it was funny that Jonathan wanted a dog so much. One sister or the other would bark like a dog, just to see what Jonathan would do. But much of the time they wished, too, that Jonathan could have a dog. They wished they could all have a dog.

One day the sisters saw a big stuffed dog in a toy store. Toni said, "Valerie, we could buy that stuffed dog for Jonathan. He will like it."

Valerie looked at the stuffed dog and said, "Toni, it looks like a real dog!"

The sisters had to carry the stuffed dog on the train. To some people, it looked like a real dog.

When the sisters gave the stuffed dog to Jonathan, he was very happy. It was almost like a real dog! It would be Jonathan's new best friend. Jonathan thought he would call the dog Fred.

Mama was pleased to see how much Jonathan's big sisters wanted to make him happy.

That night Jonathan watched TV with Fred right by him. At around eight, Jonathan was sleeping in front of the TV. Mama carried Jonathan to bed. Fred was still by the TV.

In bed that night, Mama could not sleep. "What was it that I did not do?" she thought. Then it came to her, "I did not turn off the TV!"

When Mama got out of bed and walked into the room where the TV was, she saw a dog! "We don't have a dog," she thought. Then she laughed. "It is Fred, the stuffed dog, not a real dog."

Mama looked at Fred. The stuffed dog made her think of a real dog she had when she was a girl. He was called Rusty. She had liked Rusty so much! Then Mama thought about Jonathan, Toni, and Valerie.

In the morning Jonathan, his big sisters, and Mama were eating breakfast.

"Last night, I did not turn off the TV before I went to bed," said Mama. "So I had to get up to turn it off after you were all in bed."

"Was there a good show on TV then?" asked Toni.

"There was a good show in front of the TV," said Mama. "I saw Fred and thought he was real."

"Were you afraid?" asked Valerie.

"No," said Mama, "but he made me think about Rusty, the dog I had when I was a girl. Rusty was a good dog."

"That is what Gramps used to say," said Toni.

"I thought about Gramps, too, after I went back to bed," said Mama. "He always said children should have a dog."

Jonathan, Toni, and Valerie looked at Mama. "That is why, after breakfast, we are going to get a dog, a real dog," Mama said.

Jonathan jumped up from the breakfast table and asked, "We are?"

"Yes, we will take the train to the store," said Mama.

"Thank you, Mama," said Jonathan.

That night Jonathan watched TV with Mama, his big sisters, and his two new best friends—Fred and a little puppy he called Rusty!